Who's Been Eating MY Porridge?

To Mr and Mrs Bear
and Little Bear
Woodcutter's Cottage
Leafy Lane

To Little Miss Muffet
The Tuffet
Curds and Whey Way

To Jack
Beanstalk House
Giant's Causeway

To Little Red Riding Hood
Grandma's Cottage
Deep in the Woods

To
Little Billy Goat Gruff
High Tops
Mountain Track

Who's Been Eating MY Porridge?

Nick Ward

Hippo

For Megan

Look out for:
A Wolf at the Door!

Scholastic Children's Books
Commonwealth House, 1-19 New Oxford Street
London WC1A 1NU, UK
a division of Scholastic Ltd
London ~ New York ~ Toronto ~ Sydney ~ Auckland
Mexico City ~ New Delhi ~ Hong Kong

First published in hardback in the UK by Scholastic Ltd, 2003
First published in paperback in the UK by Scholastic Ltd, 2003
This paperback edition first published in the UK by Scholastic Ltd, 2004

Copyright © Nick Ward, 2003

ISBN 0 439 98220 0

Early one morning, Little Bear
woke up with a rumble in his
tummy. He crept downstairs
as quietly as he could, but . . .

. . . when he got to the kitchen, the porridge pot was nowhere to be seen. "That's strange," said Little Bear. "Mama always leaves it ready for breakfast."

Just then, there was a
knock at the door.
Little Bear lifted the latch,
and there stood . . .

KNOCK!
KNOCK!

. . . Little Billy Goat Gruff.
"Quick, let's run," bleated
Billy. "It can't have gone far!"

"What do you mean?" asked Little Bear.
"The Porridge Monster!" cried Billy.
"Look!" and he pointed to . . .

. . . huge porridgey footsteps leading
out of the door.
"It's taken our porridge pot, too,"
explained Billy. "Come on!"

So Little Bear and Billy set off to find their porridge.

They hadn't gone far when they met Little Miss Muffet.

"Have you seen our porridge?" asked the two friends. "The Porridge Monster took it!"

"No, but you can share my curds
and whey," said Little Miss Muffet.
Little Bear's tummy rumbled.
"Yes please," he said, just as . . .

KERPLOP! A big hairy spider jumped into
Little Miss Muffet's bowl.
"Eeeek!" cried everyone, and away they
ran, over the hills and down
the lane, until they came to . . .

Yummy, breakfast!

. . . Jack's house.
"Have you seen our porridge?"
asked Little Bear and Billy. "The
big hairy Porridge Monster took it!"
"No, but you can have some
beans," said Jack.
Little Bear's tummy rumbled.
"Well," he began, when . . .

Invitation

Thump! Thump! Thump!

An enormous boot appeared at the top of the beanstalk.

"It's the giant!" yelped Jack. "Run!"
And Little Bear and Billy and Little Miss Muffet and Jack ran and ran, through the field and up to the forest, where they met . . .

. . . Little Red Riding Hood.
"Have you seen our porridge?" panted
Little Bear and Billy. "The giant hairy
Porridge Monster took it!"
"No," said Little Red Riding
Hood. "But you can have
some jam."

Where did everyone go?

Little Bear's tummy
rumbled.
"Yummy!" he said,
but then . . .

To Grandma's

. . . a terrible howling came from deep
within the forest.
"It's the big bad wolf!" cried Little Red
Riding Hood. "Run!"
And off they all ran, through the forest
and down to the stream, straight into . . .

. . . the Three Bears, who were coming home from holiday. "Have you seen our porridge?" gasped Little Bear and Billy. "The giant, hairy, howling Porridge Monster took it!"

It was only me!

"No, but you are
welcome to join us
for breakfast, dears,"
said Mother Bear.
Little Bear's tummy
rumbled.
"Thanks," he said,
when suddenly . . .

"Look!" cried Billy. "The footsteps
are back!"
"Hmmm," said Father Bear. "They
seem to be leading to . . .

. . . *my* house!"

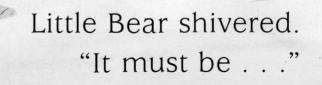

Little Bear shivered.
"It must be . . ."

...the Porridge Monster! The giant, hairy, howling, HUNGRY Porridge Monster!

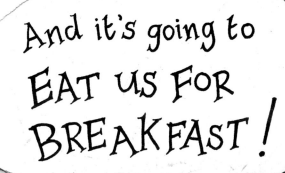

Everyone held their breath as Mother Bear reached for the door.

Slowly she turned the handle.
"Come on out, whoever you are!"
she cried, and she flung open the door
to find . . .

. . . Goldilocks, and pots and pots of steaming, sticky porridge!

"Yummy," everyone cried, "it's a porridge party!"
And monster portions of porridge were eaten
until no one could eat any more!

Dear Little Bear
Please come to an amazing
~ Porridge Party ~
to welcome home
The Three Bears
~~~~
P.S. I've borrowed your Porridge pot!
love Goldilocks X

7.00 a.m. 3 Bears Lane

Dear Little Miss Muffet
Please come to an amazing
~ Porridge Party ~
to welcome home
**The Three Bears**
~~~~
P.S. I've borrowed some bowls!
love Goldilocks X

7.00 a.m. 3 Bears Lane

Dear Jack
Please come to an amazin[g]
Porridge Party
to welcome home

Dear Little Red Riding Hood
Please come to an amazing
Porridge Party
to welcome home
The Three Bears
P.S. I've borrowed your Porridge Spoon!
7.00 a.m. 3 Bears Lane   love Goldilocks X

Dear Little Billy Goat Gruff
Please come to an amazing
Porridge Party
to welcome home
The Three Bears
P.S. I've borrowed your Porridge Pot!
[...]rs Lane   love Goldilocks X